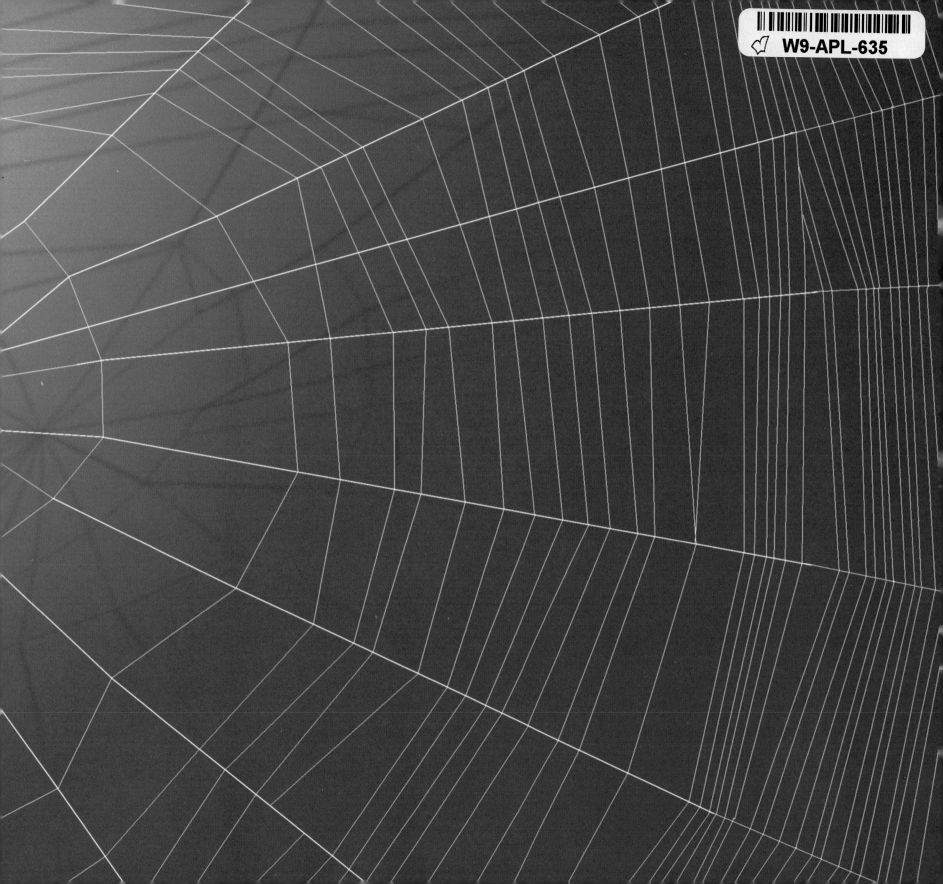

published by
BiG GUY BOOKS, Inc.
www.bigguybooks.com

| ISBN# | 1-929945-22-1 | $15.95 |

Library of Congress Cataloging-in-Publication Data Available

BiG GUY BOOKS, Inc.
7750 El Camino Real
Suite F
Carlsbad, CA 92009
www.bigguybooks.com

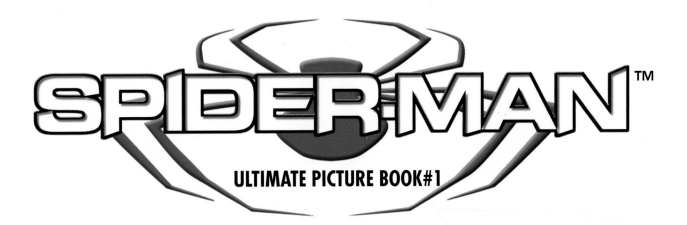

SPIDER-MAN™

ULTIMATE PICTURE BOOK#1

Published by
BiG GUY BOOKS™
www.bigguybooks.com

MARVEL™
www.marvel.com

Photographed & Directed by
ROBERT GOULD

Digital Illustrations by
EUGENE EPSTEIN

Story Boards & Casting by
RAIN RAMOS

Written by
KATHLEEN DUEY

Based upon the story and characters created by Stan Lee

FRIDAY 3:45 PM Osborn Industries

Norman Osborn was a brilliant scientist. He was rich and well known—but he was a monster inside. He founded Osborn Industries and built an incredible research lab out on Long Island. I saw it on that field trip—the one that changed my life

forever. It was a dream set-up—hot computers, molecular scopes, bio-engineering clean-rooms. Long before I saw the lab, Osborn's OZ project was all over the internet—the hackers, bio-geeks, and SF-nerds had message boards full of rumors

Most of them said that the experiments had used animals and insects—and that humans were next. But the whole thing was corrupt. Norman Osborn didn't love pure science. He never loved anything but money and power, not even his own son.

Osborn's ambition changed him into something so strange that I can barely believe it happened. No one can. That sounds crazy, I know, but it's true. I saw it. I was there.

My name is Peter Parker.

MONDAY 7:45 AM   P.S. #163 - Queens District

Harry was Mr. Cool at school. He played basketball. I always tried out, even though I stunk. But Flash Thompson was the biggest jerk—I mean star—on the team. The jocks he hung with were allergic to reading, studying, even thinking...

But they were endlessly entertained by the sight of me with french fries in my hair. Or water on my pants or, best of all, the spectacle of me sprawled flat on concrete. They were so clever. Their eraser-sized brains came up with new ways to torture me every day.

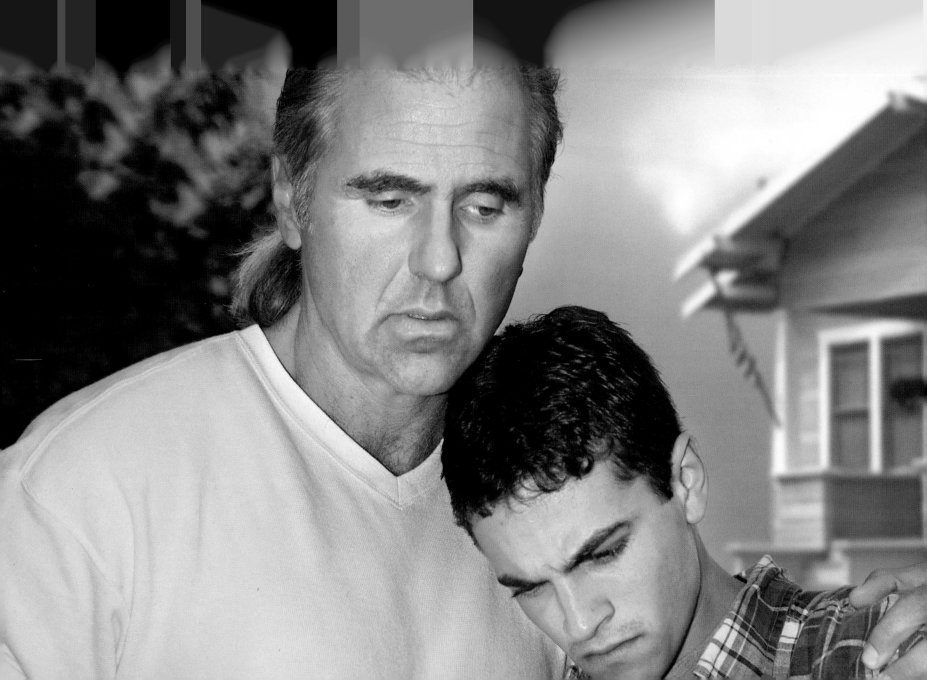

TUESDAY   11:17 AM   Field Trip - Osborn Industries - Main Lab

  The field trip changed everything. I was staring at a cool spider that was being exposed to some weird light-bath when the glass dome just exploded into a million pieces. I felt something land on my wrist..

  A pain streaked up my arm into my chest. It burned like lava in my veins. I thought I was going to die. Mary Jane kept calling my name, but all I could do was scream...then everything went dark.

TUESDAY 11:20 AM Osborn Industries

Harry told me later his dad had security cameras that taped the whole thing. I couldn't imagine what Norman Osborn was thinking then, but I can now. He was excited. For him, the accident that changed my whole life had been nothing but a lucky break.

Thanks to me being in the wrong place at the wrong time Norman Osborn wouldn't have to get government approval to experiment on humans. All he had to do was observe the results. And guess who got to be the lab rat? Yeah...me.

The next day at school I felt OK until Flash and his buddies started in on me. Flash moaned, holding his arm. The biggest guy, Kong, acted out the whole spider-bite scene, pretending to faint like I had. It really made me angry, and I tried to walk away. But then, the air started to crackle and spark. I felt hot and cold at the same time and started shaking. Everything started spinning... then the lights went out again.

Page 10 - I woke up in a hospital. They took a blood sample—but it never made it to any lab. I know where it ended up. Osborn sent someone to the hospital to intercept it. He wanted to keep close track of his human lab rat.

WEDNESDAY 4:35 PM

I don't know what Norman Osborn was thinking— or what his team of scientists saw when they tested my blood. But I know this:Osborn called in one of his men that day and gave him a very simple order—

That blood sample must have been awfully abnormal...

I felt fine by morning. I just wanted to have a normal day.

THURSDAY 7:20 AM

I started out walking fast, but the closer I got to school, the slower I went. Maybe normal wasn't so great. Flash and Kong would do their stupid fainting routines the instant they saw me and—and then my thoughts stopped.

There was complete silence inside my skull. I felt strange—not faint this time, just strong. The tension in my muscles was incredible. The air seemed different; the whole world seemed to be waiting for something to happen...

THURSDAY 7:20:02 AM

A black car screamed around the corner and the driver hit the gas, smoking the tires, aiming straight for me. I wasn't scared. How weird is that?? I rocked forward, balancing on the balls of my feet, staring at the car, feeling ready. I read once that a good hitter can see the stitching on a baseball at 85 miles an hour. It sounded impossible to me.

Guess what? It isn't.

I saw the dark brown flecks of road dust on the polished bumper as I set my foot on it and leaped upward. Then I counted six tiny scratches on the car's roof as I vaulted over it. I judged the force of the vault, too, because I wanted to land safe...

out of the street. I nailed it like an Olympic gymnast, then dropped into a crouch, ready again. The driver slammed on the brakes and jumped out. He did not look friendly. My muscles reacted instantly. I took off—faster than any normal human possibly could.

I veered down an alley, then crossed the street. I passed the pet store. They had tarantulas for sale. I bought one, then headed home. Aunt May and Uncle Ben were at work. My basement lab was quiet…peaceful…

ARACHNIDS:

Spiders are incredibly strong—some, able to lift hundreds of times their bodyweight. That would be equivalent to a human lifting several tons. All spiders produce poisonous venom. Spiders are hyper-alert to their surroundings and react to changes in air pressure, sound vibration, light changes, etc., and can often react even before the unexpected seems to happen.

The tip of the abdomen has silk spinning glands. Eggs are laid within a silken egg sac. One female may produce as many as 3,000 eggs. For a spiderling to grow, it must shed its skin.

Spiders make silk. It is secreted by the spinnerets as a liquid that hardens on air contact. Web varies in thickness and texture. Different kinds of web silk are used to build snares, webs, egg sacs, draglines and ballooning threads. Many spiders attach silk draglines to whatever surface they are on, to be ready with a lifeline if they are knocked from their perch. Some spiderlings "fly" by releasing silk strands until the wind drag lifts the silk—and the spider—into the air.

spinnerets under here (produce web threads)

orange-kneed tarantula

six-jointed leg

fangs (inject poison into prey)

house spider

garden spider

black widow spider

TUESDAY 9:18 AM

I put the tarantula in an old goldfish bowl, then booted up. An internet search for the word spider gave me a thousand sites. I picked the url's of museums and universities. *Spiders*, I learned, were Arachnids...*animals*, not insects. The descriptions of their abilities sounded weirdly familiar… One article said they could sense danger—that they had a kind of hyper-alertness. Uneasy, I hacked my way carefully into the Osborn Industries computer system. What I found was fascinating. They were trying to enhance certain

animal traits but all the specimens had died—except the spider that had bitten me. I took a deep breath. "Chill, Petey...you are not going to die..." The truth was, I felt more alive than I ever had! But it got me thinking—*that car had meant to kill me.*

It had to have been Osborn. Would he give up? "Maybe," I said aloud. "If I act normal." Trouble was, I didn't feel very normal. I kept staring at the tarantula, wondering how much we actually had in common.

THURSDAY 11:48 PM

That night I lay in bed for hours, staring up at the ceiling shadows...tense, trying to figure out what to do. I noticed a fly by the light, probably keeping warm. "You clever little thing," I whispered aloud, thinking about all the stuff I had learned on the internet.

Then the strangest feeling came over me. I blinked, staring. I wanted to catch that fly...and I knew I could if I hit the wall about seven feet up, went straight across the ceiling, then pounced...

Even as I had the thoughts, my body was moving. I ran up the wall...and stuck to it like there was no gravity.

I crawled straight up, then onto the ceiling. Trust me. That fly never had a chance.

I didn't eat it.
I let it go.
I wasn't exactly a spider, after all. I was a spider-man. "Spider-Man," I said quietly, looking around my room, enjoying the fly's-eye view. "That's me."

FRIDAY 11:20 AM

In gym class Flash kept flirting with Mary Jane. She tried to walk away, but he wouldn't let her. I told him to leave her alone and he swung at me, hard. He missed by a foot. "I don't want to fight," I told him—but in a way, I did. It didn't matter.

Flash swung again. This time it had the whole weight of his gym-rat jock's frame behind it. In that instant, my spider-changed muscles and nerves took over again. I side-stepped lightly, grabbing the punch with one hand.

I let his momentum carry him around into a most uncomfortable position.
Flash howled like a baby. Then he started yelling. "You broke my hand, Parker! You broke it!"
"I didn't want to fight," I said.

I felt sorry and glad at the same time. How many times had Flash hurt me? It felt great to be able to defend myself for once. But I didn't want to enjoy it too much—I didn't want to be a jerk like Flash.

FRIDAY 11:20 PM *Queens Recycling*

I couldn't sleep. I couldn't even lay in bed. I felt very…different. I looked out the window, then opened it, and climbed out onto the roof. A second later I jumped down into the yard, landed like a cat, then ran across the lawn. I just kept going, jumping hedges and fences, moving incredibly fast. I found a junkyard and spent hours playing. I felt like a little kid again, throwing things around, things like cars and trucks…big cars and trucks…

$10,000

THE FOLLOWING TUESDAY...

I wanted to fight someone. That sounds weird, I know, but think about it. I was the dork, remember? I was the guy everyone had pushed around since grade school. It wasn't that I wanted to hurt anyone else. I didn't, not even Flash—I just wanted to win

a fight. I just wanted to be the tough guy for once, the strong one. The WTMF Challenge was the perfect opportunity. I needed a costume, though....a latex work-out suit...and a mask. The rest was easy enough...once I got the hang of the sewing machine.

SATURDAY 8:09 PM Manhattan Sports Arena

The view from up top was great. I focused through the first few matches, watching, learning the moves. I was excited and nervous, but underneath I was calm. I felt like I did the day Osborn's driver tried to run me over. I wasn't scared. I was just...*ready.*

And then it was my turn. When they announced the contest I dropped into the ring. It was quite an entrance. The crowd went nuts. The announcer leaned toward me. "Got a ring name?"
I nodded. "Spider-Man."

He laughed. "Spiders get crushed."
I shook my head. "Not tonight they don't."
Crusher Hogan scowled at me. "Why the mask,
Spider-Man? Afraid I'll embarass you little fella?"
I didn't bother to answer —the announcer was
introducing us to the audience.
 When the bell rang, I jumped right over his head. The
crowd roared. Crusher Hogan was about to get a whole
new perspective on life.

It was cool.
It was amazing.
Crusher was huge—and he wanted to mash me like
my namesake—but he couldn't. My reactions were
too quick. It was like he was moving in slow motion.

I finally let him get close enough to think he was
about to get his hands on me at last.
Then I pulled him off balance and got under him,
lifting him over my head. He weighed in at over
300 pounds...of solid muscle. He was *not* happy.

- The other wrestlers surrounded me after the match. They wouldn't let me collect the prize money until I took off my mask. Not possible. I jumped straight up, hit the ceiling for an instant, then the far wall, then dropped down through the door. I was outta there...

SATURDAY 9:03 PM

I walked on, lost in thought. On 5th Avenue, right behind me, some guy snatched a woman's purse. He slammed into me, then dissappeared around the corner.

The woman was upset, but she wasn't hurt.

I was glad she was OK, but I kept walking. There are too many little street crimes every night in New York—but they weren't my concern.

I had my own problems.

I caught the subway to Queens and walked home

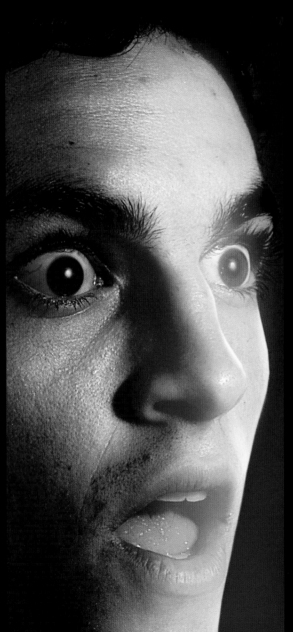

SATURDAY 9:57:00 PM My house

When I turned onto my street, I saw the flashing lights. My heart raced and a sudden cold sweat made me shiver. I walked faster, staring, squinting into the dark, hoping that the cop cars were in front of someone else's house. But they weren't. And the instant I saw Aunt May's face, I knew something terrible had happened...

SATURDAY 9:58:07 PM

"A burglar killed Ben," she said carefully, reaching out to hold my hand.

My whole system jammed. I couldn't say anything. I couldn't look at anyone. I tried to comfort Aunt May, but I could barely sit still. Mary Jane was there,

but I couldn't even talk to her, not yet. The killer was still out there...somewhere... nearby.

I could feel him. I ran out of the house.

The darkness swallowed me up.

SATURDAY 10:07:28 PM

The guy had lost his gun and found a pry-bar, a pretty nasty weapon in the right hands. I took it away from him. He tried to run—and found out that wasn't going to work, either.

Anger was exploding inside me. I wanted to hurt him.

I grabbed the front of his shirt and got in his face. I was about to tell him what a good life he had ended. I wanted him to know what a fine man my Uncle Ben had been—what a terrible thing he had done...

I couldn't speak...I couldn't breathe...because I recognized him.
Oh no...NO! How could it be the purse-snatcher? But it was.
If I had gone after him back on 5th Avenue, then he would never have...I felt my heart implode. If I had stopped the creep when I should have, Uncle Ben would still be alive.

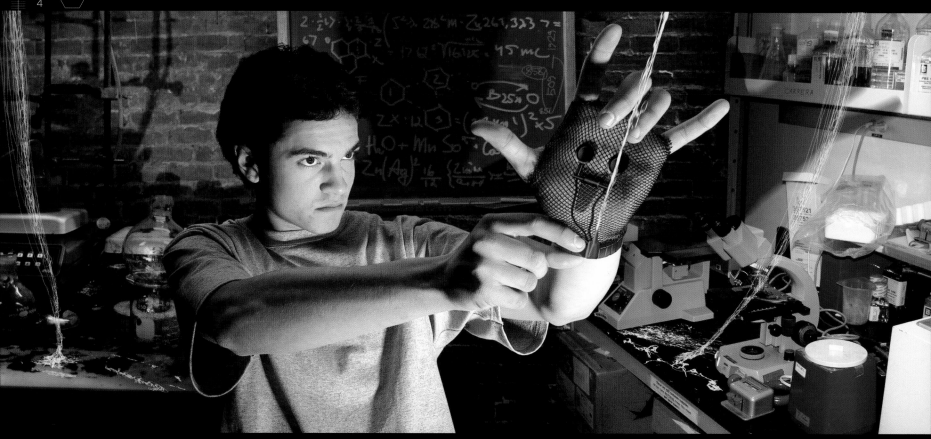

MONDAY 1:07:28 AM

Aunt May was stronger than I thought she'd be. But I think we were both in shock. We were incredibly sad. I kept hearing Uncle Ben's voice in my head. "*With great power comes great responsibility.*"
The hardest lesson of my life was in those words.
I vowed never to side-step my responsibility again.
No innocent person deserved to get hurt.
I wouldn't let it happen.
Not ever again.

And once I had made that decision, things became very simple. I knew what I had to do.

I worked in my basement lab every night. Keeping busy helped me deal with the pain of losing my Uncle Ben.
I was making breakthroughs in my experiments. I altered the chemical formula a little and my father's molecular adhesive became my secret weapon—synthetic spider web!
I designed a web-shooter that would be completely hidden by my Spider-Man costume. It was tricky, but I figured out a workable pressure system. The night I tested it outside, I was amazed. I could hit the O on the stop sign a block away.

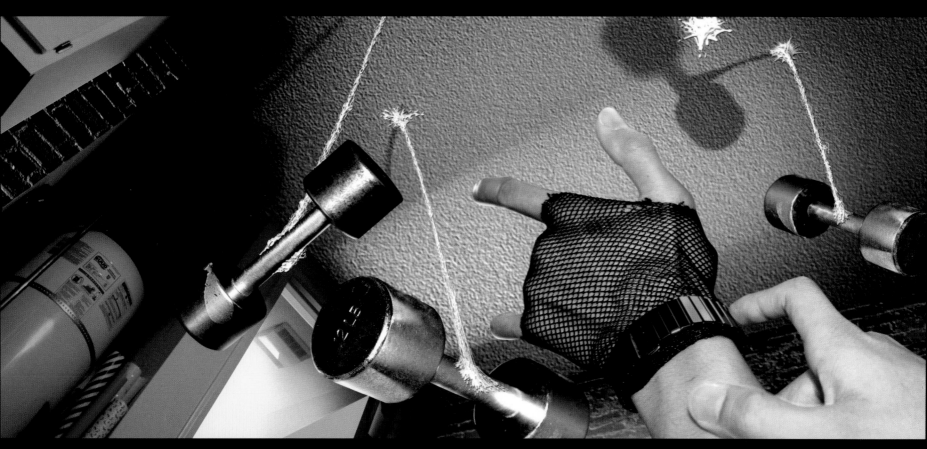

But the web wasn't strong enough. My father had been a brilliant man, but I would be using his adhesive in a way he could never have imagined. Stretch was important, but so was strength—and the liquid couldn't be too thick or it would plug up the web-shooters.

It was a balancing act. The thinner it got, the weaker it was. I started using my weights to test it and after about a hundred tries, I was getting close.

I went back to target practice. Street signs, billboards, telephone poles, nothing was too high

The stuff was amazing!

"Got web?" I whispered to myself.

"Oh yeah..."

WEDNESDAY 3:55:28 PM Back at school

I spent the rest of my nights bothering bad guys. I caught crooks, broke up muggings, prevented robberies...and I was usually half asleep in class, but I couldn't help it...
I had more important things to do.

I was worried about Harry, and I was glad the day he came back to school... We were in the cafeteria, just hanging out with everyone else, when my spider-sense started to go crazy. I knew that I needed to be ready for something big...

3:55:31 PM

About three seconds later, the air slapped against my face and exploded in my ears like a thunderclap. It was chaos. Smoke billowed into the room and people began to run. I watched to make sure Mary Jane was on her way to safety.

3:56:42 PM

Then I looked around for a place to change clothes—and identities...

3:55:00 PM

People were running in every direction. I spotted Mary Jane going out the emergency exit. She was safe for now. Then I saw it...

It was like a special effects monster...except this wasn't a movie. It was huge, and it smelled horrible, like burning sulfur mixed with sewage. The smoke was thick...choking.

It turned to face me. Every muscle tensed as my body prepared for a life-or-death battle.

I could hear Harry shouting something...

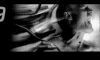

11:58:03 AM

Then his voice rose to a scream. "He's coming for me,"
Poor Harry. He'd had such a lousy family life that he
thought everything bad was a special delivery package—
addressed to him.
And this one was. My spider-sense was raging.

This thing was pure evil.
I had beaten Crusher Hogan. I had faced street-
tough muggers and cold-hearted killers in the city
every night. I had been pretty sure I would never
feel real fear again. Yeah. Well. Never say never.

3:58:14 PM

Its arms were like pistons as it came toward me, hurling fireballs. I dodged as they flew past, blasting through the wall behind me. The heat and the sharp sulfur stink burned my lungs...

I staggered back, watching its moves...preparing. It looked past me for a second, and I attacked, hitting hard. A man would have fallen dead. Concrete would have shattered. But the thing just kept coming at me...

I kept going, jumping from one building to the next, trying to lure it away from the city. Fire streamed from its hands. Its eyes glowed like some sort of nightmarish goblin. But it looked like a man...so maybe I could knock it out...

4:33:17 PM

I slammed every ounce of spider-strength I had against that huge , ugly green chin. For a second I thought I'd finally hit the monster hard enough. I let myself believe it'd end up on its back like all the alley-crooks I'd fought.

But I was about as far wrong as a spider-guy could be. The goblin thing stood up and came at me again. I could hear cars honking...and helicopters. I wanted to run away. Then I remembered Uncle Ben, and knew I couldn't...running away is not my job.

6:38:22 PM

I struggled but its grip was suffocating, bone cracking. We went out over the park, then veered toward the water.

"Paaarkerrrrr."

The air-brake hiss of the goblin's voice horrified me.

How could it possibly know my name? How????
In that instant its grip loosened. I glanced at the bridge hundreds of feet below.

Then the monster dropped me.

4:38:33 PM

I plunged down, the wind shrieking in my ears, fireballs hurtling towards me. Things weren't looking real good for Peter Parker—but I knew this much: Spiders rarely fall to the ground.

There is usually some wisp of a leaf, some tiny twig they can use.

In my case, it was the Brooklyn Bridge.

4:38:35 PM

Spiders hate water. So I ran a little real-time experiment...I extended my right arm and aimed at the bridge tower. I watched the web arc out...and stick...and hold!!!

I grinned, wishing my father could have seen his theories in action. A second later, I heard helicopters.

it flailed and spun, throwing fireballs. The pilots pulled back—chopper blades are fragile. Finally, I swung in a tight circle and slammed it as hard as I could. It was beginning to weaken.

5:22:16 PM

"Get down and put your hands behind your head!"
I knew they were just doing their job, but they
didn't understand what I was…and I knew I could
never explain it.
  I glanced once more at the churning water.

  The goblin was gone. I fired a strand of web and
jumped. I swung a beautiful seventy-foot arc and
landed up-side-down beneath the bridge. I hid there
until the police finally gave up looking for me. I
had time to do some thinking.

9:18:02 PM

I stood on the roof, trying to feel like a 16 year old high school student again...
"My father is coming for me!"
It was Harry's voice... I glanced down. He was still in the street, still wandering. Harry Osborn...my best friend. His words sank in, and I shuddered.
It made a sad and terrible kind of sense.
The Green Goblin had once been Norman Osborn— the monster inside him had finally come out.

I pulled off my mask...
Everyone my age wonders what life will be like. But I wasn't going to have a life. I was going to have two...

Spider-Man had done his job. He'd be back. But it was time for me to do Peter's work. I had to find Aunt May and Mary Jane and let them know I was OK.

I'd figure the rest out later.

CAST

Peter Parker/Spiderman	**Raphael Arcuri**
Norman Osborn	**Mark Flanagan**
Goblin	**Kenneth Etta**
Mary Jane	**Hayley Jean**
Uncle Ben	**Christopher Miller**
Aunt May	**JoAnn Schmied**
Flash Thompson	**Michael Cummings**
Harry Osborn	**Matt Margolin**
Crusher Hogan	**Nate Brock**
Kong	**Ron Padua**
Robber	**Kennedy Carr**
Liz	**Ryan Israel**
Mugged Woman	**Mary Sarlo**
Head Scientist	**Stan Lee**
Scientists	**Kenneth Wolff,**
	Rebecca Levas
Henchmen	**Bob Wells, John Mannion,**
	John Pina, Brett Russell

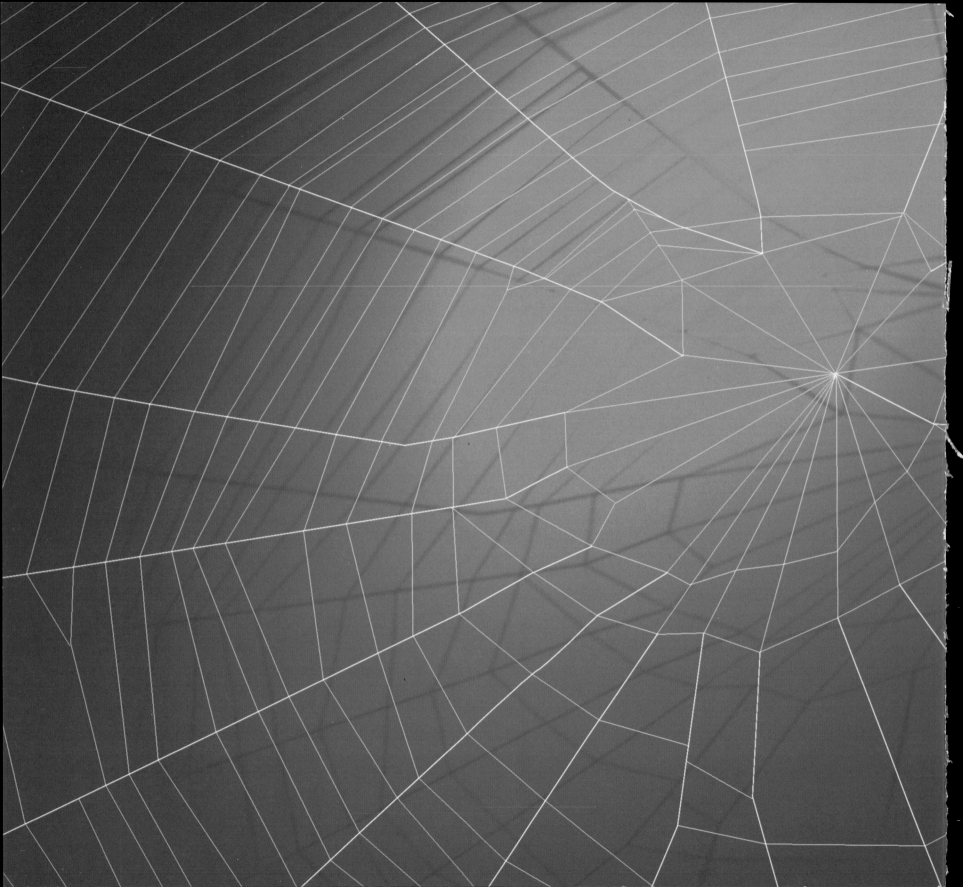